A Note from Michelle about My Best Friend Is a Movie Star!

Hi! I'm Michelle Tanner. I'm nine years old. And the coolest, most exciting thing just happened to me!

I met Natalie Campbell—a real live movie star! I couldn't wait to get back to school and tell everyone I was friends with someone famous.

But no one believed me! So I came up with a plan to prove it. The plan would take a lot of work. But that was no problem. My house is crammed with people willing to help me. There's my dad and my two older sisters, D.J. and Stephanie. But that's not all.

My mom died when I was little. So my uncle Jesse moved in to help Dad take care of us. So did Joey Gladstone. He's my dad's friend from college. It's almost like having three dads. But that's still not all!

First Uncle Jesse got married to Becky Donaldson. Then they had twin boys, Nicky and Alex. The twins are four years old now. And they're so cute.

That's nine people. Our dog, Comet, makes ten. Sure, it gets kind of crazy sometimes. But I wouldn't change it for anything. It's so much fun to live in a full house!

FULL HOUSE™ MICHELLE novels

The Great Pet Project
The Super-Duper Sleepover Party
My Two Best Friends
Lucky, Lucky Day
The Ghost in My Closet
Ballet Surprise
Major League Trouble
My Fourth-Grade Mess
Bunk 3, Teddy and Me
My Best Friend Is a Movie Star!
The Big Turkey Escape
The Substitute Teacher
Calling All Planets
I've Got a Secret
How to Be Cool

Available from MINSTREL Books

FULL HOUSE™ Michelle

My Best Friend Is a Movie Star!

Cathy East Dubowski

A Parachute Press Book

Published by POCKET BOOKS
New York London Toronto Sydney Tokyo Singapore

A MINSTREL PAPERBACK *Original*

A Minstrel Book published by
POCKET BOOKS, a division of Simon & Schuster Inc.
1230 Avenue of the Americas, New York, NY 10020

A PARACHUTE PRESS BOOK

ISBN: 0-671-56835-3

First Minstrel Books printing September 1996

10 9 8 7 6 5 4

Cover photo by Schultz Photography

Printed in the U.S.A.

My Best Friend
Is a Movie Star!

Chapter 1

Michelle Tanner sat on the beach under a sunny, blue sky. The sparkling ocean water splashed inches away from her toes.

The temperature? Good and warm, with a gentle breeze. Absolutely perfect.

The *whole day* was absolutely perfect.

Michelle buried her bare feet in the sand and frowned. Because one tiny little thing ruined it all. Michelle was absolutely, 100 percent *bored!*

She wanted to complain to her father, but didn't. She already knew what he would say: "Only boring people get bored."

She glanced at him. Danny Tanner sat on

the deck of the beach cottage they were renting. His new cookbook lay open on his lap. What did he know about being nine years old and bored out of your mind?

And D.J., her eighteen-year-old sister, was no better. Look how she was spending their special long-weekend getaway in Carmel! Stretched out on her stomach on a beach towel—studying for a history test. That was no fun!

Michelle's thirteen-year-old sister, Stephanie, was no fun, either. She had plunked herself down in a beach chair under a huge, striped beach umbrella.

Michelle shook her head. How can Stephanie even tell she's at the beach? Michelle thought. She can't see the ocean—she has her nose stuck in a Hollywood gossip magazine. She can't even hear the waves—she has her Walkman on.

Too bad we couldn't bring our dog, Comet. At least he would have dug in the sand with me, Michelle thought. But the cottage rules said "No Dogs Allowed." So Comet had to stay home with Joey, her dad's best friend, who lived with the Tanners.

Even Uncle Jesse and Aunt Becky's four-year-old twin boys—Nicky and Alex—would have been some company, Michelle thought. But the twins were both home with the chicken pox!

Michelle sighed and jumped to her feet. She couldn't sit here all day, waiting for something to happen. "Dad—can I take a walk down the beach?" Michelle asked.

"Uh-huh," Danny called back from the deck, his eyes glued to his cookbook. "But don't wander too far."

Michelle wrapped her beach towel over her shoulders like a cape. She slipped on her hot-pink flip-flops, picked up a bucket for shells, and headed down the beach.

As she walked along the water's edge, an old stick washed ashore. The ocean had worn it smooth. Michelle picked it up and drew a huge face in the sand. She gave it a great big frown. Under the face, she wrote in big loopy letters as tall as she was: Michelle Tanner is B O R E D ! ! !

That took about three minutes, Michelle thought. Now what should I do?

Then she got an idea! She dashed back to the cottage. "Dad, can I have your empty juice bottle?"

Danny turned a page in his cookbook. "Sure, honey," he said without taking his eyes off the recipe. "Just be careful. We don't want any broken glass around all these bare feet."

Michelle rolled her eyes and grabbed the bottle. Her dad was Mr. Safety—even on vacation. "Thanks, Dad."

Next she ran over to D.J. "Can I have paper and a pen?"

"Whatever," D.J. said without looking up.

"Thanks." Michelle tore a sheet of paper from D.J.'s notebook. On it she wrote:

Dear Anyone!

HELP! I am trapped on a deserted island. I am totally bored! Save me!

Best wishes,
Michelle Tanner, age 9

Grinning, she rolled up the note. Wait! she thought. Better write down my address. She unrolled the paper and wrote down "Laughing Gull Cottage."

Then she rolled the note back up and stuffed it into the bottle. She screwed the cap on tight.

Michelle ran down the beach. She didn't want D.J. or Stephanie to see what she was doing. If they did, they would tease her for the rest of the weekend.

Michelle twirled around seven times—for good luck. She hopped on each foot seven times—for extra good luck. Then she flung the bottle as hard as she could straight into the ocean.

Now I just have to wait for someone to

get my message, she thought. Maybe it will be somebody from the other side of the ocean. Maybe a kid from Japan. That would be so cool!

Michelle headed up the beach and plopped down in the warm sand. She dropped her bucket next to her. She watched the waves sparkle in the sunshine. *I wonder how long it takes a bottle to float all the way to Japan. . . .*

Michelle sighed. This was totally silly. Of course nobody would find her message right away. It might take hours. Maybe even days! She would be long gone by then, back home in San Francisco. *Or maybe my stupid bottle already sank to the bottom of the ocean. Maybe it's in the stomach of some octopus right now.*

Michelle stretched out in the sand and listened to the waves splash on the shore. The warm sun made her sleepy. She closed her eyes and slept—until she felt somebody poke her foot.

"Hi! Is this bottle yours?"

Chapter 2

♡ Michelle's eyes snapped open. She squinted in the bright sunlight.

A girl with long blond hair, green eyes, and a pug nose covered with freckles stood in front of her. She wore an Animaniacs T-shirt over her bathing suit, and she held a purple bucket in one hand.

Michelle jumped up. "Are you from Japan?" she asked.

The girl laughed. "No. But I'm from L.A. Does that count?"

Michelle felt her face get hot. I can't believe I said that, she thought.

"I found this bottle. Is it yours? Are you Michelle? My name is Natalie."

"Yes!" Michelle exclaimed. "Where did you find it?"

"I saw you throw something into the water," Natalie explained. "A few minutes later this bottle washed up near me. I read the note and guessed you were the one who wrote it."

"I did! I was hoping it would float all the way to Japan. I thought a Japanese girl would find it and write me back," she admitted. "I guess my experiment was a big fat failure."

"Maybe not," Natalie said.

"What do you mean?" Michelle asked.

"I'm here to save you."

"Save me from what?"

Natalie giggled. "Don't you remember?" She unrolled Michelle's note. "Your note says 'I am totally bored! Save me!' "

"Oh, right," Michelle said, embarrassed. It sounded kind of dumb now.

"Well, maybe we could save each other," Natalie said. "Because I feel the same way."

"You do?"

"Uh-huh." Natalie pointed down the beach. "Look."

Michelle could see two people sitting in beach chairs—a man, who was asleep, and a woman reading a fat paperback.

"Those are my parents," Natalie told her. "They said we were coming to Carmel to get away from it all."

Michelle laughed. "Grown-up talk for 'sit around and do nothing.' "

"Exactly." Natalie grinned. "I'm bored too. Do you want to hang out and be bored together?"

"Great!" Michelle said. They ran down to the water's edge and kicked their way through the white foam.

Natalie scooped up some wavy brown seaweed and draped it over her head. "Like my new wig?" she asked.

"Very cool," Michelle answered. "Hey! Let's make a mermaid out of sand. We can use that seaweed for hair."

Natalie dug around in her bucket. She pulled out two big clam shells. "These would make a great bikini top," she said.

"Yeah," Michelle agreed. She bent down and used her bucket to scoop up some wet sand. She hauled it to a flat, dry spot and dumped it.

Natalie raced over and piled her shells near the mound of wet sand. Then she and Michelle went to work on their mermaid.

"I'll start on the tail," Natalie volunteered. She dropped onto her knees and began molding the wet sand.

Michelle worked on the top half of the sand sculpture. "Let's make our mermaid as big as a car!"

"Awesome!" Natalie answered.

This is what a day at the beach should be like, Michelle thought. Not sitting around reading or sleeping or doing homework. That note in the bottle turned out to be a great idea.

"Want to switch?" Natalie asked.

"Okay." Michelle scooted down to the mermaid's tail. She picked out a whole bunch of tiny shells from Natalie's collection and used them for tail scales.

Natalie stuck on the seaweed hair, and the clam shell bathing suit top. Then she made the mermaid a pair of long dangly earrings out of shiny pebbles.

"Our mermaid is totally incredible," Michelle said. "What should we name her?"

"How about . . ." Natalie thought a minute. "Myrtle!"

Michelle scrunched up her nose. "Myrtle?"

"Sure! Myrtle the Mermaid." Natalie giggled. "Don't you think she looks like a Myrtle?"

Michelle studied the mermaid. "Yeah! You're right. And look at this!" She mounded up some wet sand a few feet away. "The perfect pet."

"Myrtle's turtle!" Natalie shrieked.

Quickly she added a leash and collar of shells.

The girls stood up and admired their artwork. "We need to get a picture of this," Michelle said.

"I'll get my mom! She takes great pictures." Natalie raced down the beach. A few minutes later she returned with her mom and a camera.

"This is Lara," Natalie said.

"Hi!" Natalie's mom smiled at Michelle.

How cool to call your mother by her first name, Michelle thought.

Lara was tall and slim, with blond hair and green eyes, just like Natalie's. She wore a faded T-shirt over her swimsuit. She looked like a model. She was beautiful!

"This is fabulous!" Lara said when she spotted their mermaid. "Girls, I'm impressed."

Michelle and Natalie grinned. "Sit behind the mermaid," Lara instructed. "Then I can get the ocean in the picture too."

The girls plopped down in the sand and put their arms across each other's shoulders.

Lara held up her camera. "Say cheese!"

"Cheeeeeese!" the girls shouted.

Lara smiled. "We'll send you a copy of the picture when we get it developed," she told Michelle. "Be sure to give Natalie your address."

Michelle jumped up and brushed the sand off her legs. "I'm starving," she announced. "Can Natalie come over for lunch? Our cabin is right over there." Michelle pointed down the beach.

"Well . . . I don't mind," Lara said. "But we don't want to make extra work for your folks while they are on vacation."

Michelle grabbed Natalie's hand and pulled her up. "It's just my dad. And it's no problem. He *loves* to cook. Come on!"

Michelle led the way back to their cottage. "Hey, Dad!" she yelled. "We have company for lunch."

Danny smiled as Michelle walked up with

Natalie and Lara. Lara stared at him. "Haven't I seen you somewhere before?"

"He's on TV!" Michelle bragged. "He's on *Wake Up, San Francisco.*" Michelle was proud of Danny. And his producer—Aunt Becky!

While Danny and Lara talked, Michelle took Natalie into the kitchen. "People are always recognizing my dad," Michelle said. "It's so cool that he's on TV."

"Yeah," Natalie answered.

Michelle opened the cabinets and looked inside. "Dad can make us something for lunch. But most stuff he cooks takes a lot of time. How about peanut butter and jelly? It's faster."

Natalie grinned. "Fast is good. I'm starving too."

Michelle and Natalie made their sandwiches, and grabbed a couple slices of watermelon from the fridge. They took their lunch out on the deck to eat.

"Hey, my dad's here," Natalie said. "I

guess he finally woke up!" She rolled her eyes at Michelle.

Michelle giggled. Natalie's dad wore a neon orange shirt, tan pants, and sandals. He had his hair pulled back into a short little ponytail.

Michelle took a big bite of watermelon. Mmmm, sweet and juicy. She leaned forward and spit the seeds off the deck. Natalie spit out her seeds too—and one of them landed on Stephanie's bare foot!

Stephanie turned around and gave them both a disgusted look. Michelle and Natalie cracked up.

Michelle took another big bite. Then she spit the seeds right at Natalie! One of them got stuck in Natalie's blond hair.

"Watermelon fight!" Natalie cried. She shot her seeds at Michelle.

This is so great! Michelle thought. A few hours ago this trip was a total bomb. Now she was having a ball!

By the time they were finished with lunch,

both girls' hair dripped watermelon. So they raced into the ocean and rinsed it out. Then they used Michelle's red and blue raft to ride the waves.

That evening, Danny invited Natalie to stay for a barbecue. And after that, he took them over to a nearby amusement park to watch a fireworks display.

The perfect end to a perfect day, Michelle thought.

The next day Natalie's family had to leave for home. But Natalie promised Michelle she would write.

"I may not be Japanese," Natalie joked, "but I can still be your pen pal." They exchanged addresses and phone numbers.

Michelle and Natalie hugged good-bye. Michelle waved until their car disappeared from view. Then she walked back to her cottage. She sat down on one of the wooden deck chairs and sighed.

Danny glanced up from his reading. *Another* cookbook. "You miss Natalie, huh?"

"Yeah. We had such a great time. I wish she didn't have to leave so soon."

Danny nodded. "When we get home you can use my computer to write her a letter. I'll show you how to put pictures in it and everything."

"Thanks," Michelle mumbled.

"And who knows," Danny said, "maybe you and Natalie will have a chance to get together again."

But in her heart Michelle knew the truth. She would probably never ever see Natalie again in her whole life!

Chapter 3

Michelle started planning her first letter to Natalie as the Tanners drove home. I want to put in a picture of Comet, she thought. And—

Suddenly Stephanie gasped. She grabbed Michelle's arm. "Michelle! It's your friend!"

"Where?" Michelle cried. "Which car?"

"No! No!" Stephanie shook her glossy magazine in front of Michelle's face.

"Huh?" Michelle stared at it. *People* magazine. "Stephanie, what are you talking about?"

"Here!" Stephanie shoved the magazine into Michelle's hands. "Look!"

Michelle stared down at the big photo. "It-it *is* Natalie! But she looks so different."

Natalie had her hair up, and she was wearing dark red lipstick. She looked older—not at all like the girl Michelle met at the beach.

D.J. leaned over the front seat. "What is Natalie doing in *People* magazine?"

"I don't know!" Michelle answered.

"Well, read it!" Stephanie cried. "What does it say?"

Michelle began to read the article.

"I meant read it out loud!" Stephanie grabbed the magazine back. "Listen." She began to read:

" 'Natalie Campbell may be one of the greatest young actresses to come along in years. She's fresh, natural, and totally believable.' Blah, blah, blah . . .

" 'Natalie Campbell. Remember the name. You'll definitely be seeing her at next year's Academy Awards show.' "

"I don't understand!" Michelle cried. "I

go to a lot of movies. And I never heard of her!"

"Me either," Stephanie said. "It says she's had parts in some plays on Broadway. And she's been in two movies: *McLeary's End* and *Frenzied.*"

"I saw those," Danny called from the front seat. "They were movies for grown-ups. But I don't remember . . . Oh, wait! Did she play the little girl Susie in *Frenzied*?"

Stephanie searched the article. "Yes! That was her!"

"Amazing," Danny said as he turned the corner. "She was excellent! But she was a lot younger then. Maybe only five or six."

"But why didn't she tell me?" Michelle asked. "Why didn't she tell me she was a movie star?"

Danny checked his rearview mirror, then turned onto the interstate. "Maybe she didn't want to brag. You don't just walk up to somebody and say, 'Hi, I'm a movie star.' "

Michelle shook her head. "And *I* was bragging to *her* because my dad's on a dinky local TV show!"

"Hey! What do you mean—a dinky local TV show?" Danny exclaimed.

"Listen to this," Stephanie interrupted. " 'Natalie's mother is Lara Leigh, who was a top model and part-time actress before she married Roger Campbell and retired.' "

That explains why she looked like a model, Michelle thought. She *was* a model!

" 'Her father is Broadway director Roger Campbell.' "

"He's that Roger Campbell?" Danny asked excitedly.

Stephanie kept reading. " 'The critics are expecting her new movie to make Natalie one of the biggest new stars in Hollywood.' "

Michelle sank down in her seat. "Oh, no . . ."

Stephanie stared at her sister as if she were crazy. "What do you mean oh, no? Michelle, you're friends with a movie star!"

"I know!" Michelle groaned. "But don't you see? I treated her like a regular kid. I gave her a plain old peanut butter and jelly sandwich for lunch. And I spit watermelon seeds in her hair!"

D.J. laughed. "So maybe she likes peanut butter and jelly and spitting watermelon seeds."

Michelle shook her head. "My one chance to be friends with a movie star—and I acted like a total geek!"

Chapter 4

♥ Danny stopped for gas, and Stephanie and Michelle ran for the Quickmart. Michelle grabbed three magazines: *Movieline, Hollywood Hotline,* and *Inside Hollywood.*

"Oh, no!" Michelle cried. "There are articles about Natalie in all of these. But I only have five dollars of my vacation spending money left."

"I'll pay half," Stephanie volunteered. She handed Michelle five dollars. "I want to read them too."

"Great!" Michelle brought them over to the teenage boy behind the counter. He ran them over the scanner. "That's nine dollars and ninety-five cents," he said.

These magazines weren't cheap! The boy took her money and stuck the magazines in a plastic bag.

"I know Natalie Campbell," Michelle bragged.

The cashier popped his gum. "Yeah, right."

"Let's go, girls," Danny called. "We've still got a long drive ahead of us."

Michelle and Stephanie pored over the magazines on the drive home. D.J. had one of those battery-operated book lights, so they could still read when it got dark.

Each magazine said the same thing. Natalie Campbell was a fabulous young actress on her way to being a major movie star!

This is so cool! Michelle thought. Now that she was used to the idea, she was starting to get excited. *I know a real live movie star! Just wait till I tell Cassie and Mandy!*

It was too late to call her friends when

they got home. But Uncle Jesse, Aunt Becky, and Joey were still up watching the news in the living room. Comet barked, happy to have them home.

Michelle hugged Comet. "Guess what, everybody?"

"What?" Joey, Becky, and Jesse asked together.

Michelle put her sunglasses on—even though it was night and she was indoors. She strutted up and down the room. "I," she said in a loud voice, "spent my vacation with a movie star."

"Ha, ha," Joey said. "What's the joke?"

"No joke," D.J. replied. "She *really* met a movie star."

"Did you get his autograph?" Aunt Becky asked.

"Hardly, darling." Michelle stuck her nose in the air and put her hands on her hips. "It is so uncool to ask your friends for autographs. And it was a she, not a he."

Everybody laughed.

"So who was it?" Jesse asked. "Anybody we know?"

"Her!" Stephanie squealed.

Michelle whirled around.

Stephanie pointed at the TV. The all-news channel's "Sixty Seconds with the Stars" spot had just come on.

"It's Natalie!" Michelle cried.

Flashbulbs popped as reporters swarmed around her. "Child actor Natalie Campbell was all smiles tonight when she showed up at the premiere of her new film *Heartbreaker."*

Natalie wore a long green dress that made her green eyes sparkle. Her long blond hair was swept into a beautiful French braid. She looked so elegant! Just like a . . .

Like a movie star, Michelle thought. What else?

Everybody started talking at once. Michelle couldn't hear what the announcer said next. She stared at the film clips of her friend flashing across the TV screen.

A very young Natalie onstage in a play.

A young Natalie asleep on her father's shoulder at some fancy New York party.

An older Natalie blowing out birthday candles at Planet Hollywood—with famous stars all around her.

Michelle had a funny feeling in the pit of her stomach. Like butterflies and the flu all mixed up.

She knew Natalie. They hung out together. But this Natalie on TV . . . She was a stranger.

Michelle felt as if she didn't really know her at all.

At school on Monday Michelle's teacher, Mrs. Yoshida, called the roll. Then she asked, "Did everyone have a good weekend? Any news to share with the class?"

Michelle almost jumped out of her seat, waving her hand.

Mrs. Yoshida laughed. "Okay, Michelle. You go first. It must be something great!"

"Oh, it is!" Michelle exclaimed. She

dashed to the front of the room. She bounced from foot to foot. She felt so excited she didn't know what to say first.

Everyone stared at her. "So what is it?" Jeff Farrington called out. "You look like you won a million dollars or something."

Everybody laughed. Jeff was always making jokes.

"I met a movie star this weekend!" Michelle blurted out.

"Really?" Cassie exclaimed.

"Who?" Mandy cried.

"Natalie Campbell!" Michelle told them.

"Who?" her friend Lee demanded. He didn't sound impressed.

"I never heard of her either," someone else said.

Michelle rolled her eyes. "Natalie Campbell! Don't you know anything? She's going to be famous as soon as *Heartbreaker* comes out. That's the movie with Brad Pitt and Winona Ryder."

"Oh, yeah! Now I know who she is. I saw

a commercial for that!" Amber Jacobson said.

"She's in a movie with Brad Pitt? That's so cool!" Mandy said.

"How did you meet her?" Cassie asked.

"My family and I went to Carmel this weekend," Michelle explained. "And I met her playing on the beach."

"Not many people have the chance to make friends with a movie star. What was she like?" Mrs. Yoshida asked.

"She was really nice," Michelle told them. "Lots of fun. And, well, just an ordinary kid, I guess."

"Ordinary!" Jeff exclaimed. "Ha! I saw her on TV last night. She didn't look ordinary to me. She lives in a mansion!"

Everybody started talking at once.

"Is she rich?"

"Did you get her autograph?"

"Does she have her own chauffeur?"

Michelle answered questions until Mrs. Yoshida said it was time for math.

At lunch kids from some of the other classes hurried over to Michelle's table. "We heard you met a movie star," one girl said.

"Yeah!" Michelle began. "She was so—"

"Michelle, want to trade my tuna sandwich for your stuffed pita bread?" Lee interrupted.

"No way. Eat your own lunch," Michelle answered.

"I don't believe you met a movie star at all," said fifth-grader Arlene Higgins.

"Come on, Michelle," Lee interrupted again. "Your dad makes the best lunches. Please."

"Why don't you believe I met a movie star?" Michelle ignored Lee. "It's true." She took a bite of Danny's special fruit salad.

"She's just jealous," Cassie whispered in Michelle's ear. "Ignore her."

"Yeah—I don't believe it either! How come her bodyguards let you get near her?" asked a boy Michelle didn't know.

"Can I have some fruit salad?" Lee interrupted for the third time.

"Lee!" Michelle exclaimed. "Aren't you interested in hearing about Natalie—a real live movie star?"

"Nah," Lee said. "I'm more interested in eating lunch. Your lunch."

"Well, what about the bodyguards?" the boy asked again. "Where were they?"

"Bodyguards?" Michelle said. "She didn't have bodyguards. She was just playing by herself on the beach."

"That proves it," Arlene said. "Movie stars don't run around by themselves like that. It's not safe."

"I bet you're making it up," José Sanchez said.

"I am not!" Michelle snapped.

But it was no use. A lot of the kids started teasing her. They kept saying there was no way Michelle hung out with a real movie star.

"I really did meet her!" Michelle insisted.

"Oh, yeah?" José jeered. He waved his sandwich in her face. "You're like my sandwich—full of baloney!"

I've got to prove it to them! Michelle thought. But *how?*

Chapter 5

SLAM! Michelle banged the front door shut when she came home from school. But it didn't make her feel any better.

She dropped her backpack and flopped down on the couch. Comet jumped up and gave her face a big lick. Even that didn't help.

"Nobody believes I know Natalie!" she complained to the big furry dog. "And Lee, one of my best friends, doesn't even care!"

Comet barked.

"Thanks, boy. But, Comet—what am I going to do?" Michelle propped her feet up on the coffee table. Then she noticed the pile of mail right next to her blue high-tops.

There was a thin FedEx package—addressed to her! Wow! Michelle had never gotten an overnight package before. She snatched it up and ripped it open. A photo fell into her lap.

It was the picture of her and Natalie next to Myrtle the Mermaid. The one with their arms around each other's shoulders.

Michelle quickly read the note:

Hi, Michelle!

I couldn't wait to get this developed! Mom took me by one of those one-hour film places on the way home. I stuck it in the mail so you could get it right away. Hope you like the picture!

I had fun making that mermaid with you!

Well, gotta go. I'll write more later! I've got to get ready to go somewhere.

Natalie

No kidding! Michelle thought. Somewhere like a big, fancy Hollywood party.

Michelle stared at the photo. What a great picture! She knew she would treasure it forever.

But even better— *Yes!* It was the proof she needed. The proof that she knew Natalie!

She passed the picture around at supper. Nicky and Alex stared at it forever. They didn't really understand who Natalie was. But they loved Myrtle and her turtle.

"You ought to frame that," Uncle Jesse said. He passed the photo to Joey and the peas to D.J.

"And the letter too," Joey added. "It might be worth something one day."

It's worth something already, Michelle thought, grinning. Just wait till I show the kids at lunch tomorrow!

The next day at school everyone heard that Michelle had a picture with Natalie Campbell—and she planned to show it at lunch. A crowd gathered at Michelle's table.

"Hey, Tanner!" said José. "We heard you have proof that you know Natalie Campbell."

"So let's see it," Arlene said.

"Okay," Michelle said. "Take a look at this!" She pulled the letter out of her backpack. She opened it.

The photo was gone!

"Uh, just a minute," she said. She dug in her backpack. It wasn't there.

At least I have the letter, Michelle thought. She handed it to José. "I got this from Natalie yesterday. That proves I know her."

"Now you've even got her autograph," Mandy said.

Arlene grabbed the letter. "So where is the picture you've been bragging about?" she demanded.

"Um, I must have left it at home."

"Aw, I bet there is no picture," José said. "And I bet this letter's a fake too. I bet you wrote it yourself!"

"I did not!" Michelle snapped.

"She wouldn't do that," Cassie said.

Michelle grabbed her friend Lee's empty lunchbag. She copied one of the sentences from the letter. Then she held up the bag. "See? My handwriting doesn't match."

"Your sister probably wrote it for you," Arlene said.

The bell rang and Michelle stomped back to class. She was so mad she could hardly concentrate on her spelling test.

Some of these kids wouldn't believe me if I showed them Natalie in person! she thought.

Wait! That gave her an idea. A great idea.

It's so simple, Michelle thought. *I'll invite Natalie to spend the weekend with me! Then I'll tell everyone to come over and meet her. Then they'll have to believe me.*

She asked her dad as soon as he got home that night. "Can she come? Please? Please? Pleaaaase?"

"Okay, honey," Danny said. "It's fine with me."

"Really?" Michelle cried.

"Sure." Danny shrugged. "Natalie is a nice girl. And I liked her parents too. Even if they are celebrities!" he joked.

"All *right!*" Michelle whooped.

Danny dialed the number. Michelle crowded close to him. She couldn't wait to find out if Natalie could come.

Her father hung up the phone after a few minutes. "Lara said Natalie was out with her father, but that she would probably love to spend the weekend with us. Lara promised to call later and let us know."

Michelle waited and waited for the phone call, but it didn't come. Finally Danny told her it was time for bed.

Michelle couldn't fall asleep. It would be so great to see Natalie again, she thought.

And prove to Arlene and José and everyone else that she really did know a real live movie star.

She finally started to doze off when she heard the phone ring. A couple minutes later her father came upstairs.

"Michelle," he whispered. "Are you awake?"

"Yes," Michelle whispered back, careful not to wake Stephanie in her bed across the room.

Danny tiptoed over and sat on the edge of her bed. "That was Lara," he told her. "Natalie can't get here Friday night—"

"Oh, no!" Michelle wailed.

"But," Danny went on, "she *can* come Saturday afternoon and spend the night. Her parents will be in town for a business meeting. How's that?"

Michelle threw her arms around her dad. "That's great!"

Danny tucked her back in and kissed her on the cheek. "Now, get to sleep. We'll make plans for Natalie's visit in the morning."

Danny left, and Michelle snuggled down

into the covers. This is going to be the best weekend ever, she thought. Now she didn't need the picture. She would have the real live movie star to show them.

But then Michelle began to worry.

She kept thinking about the big stars Natalie knew. The glamorous parties she went to.

Natalie's not an ordinary girl like me, Michelle thought.

Sure they had fun that one afternoon at the beach. But Natalie was famous. She had famous parents. She was used to Broadway theaters and Hollywood parties.

How was plain old Michelle going to top that?

Chapter 6

Michelle clicked "save" on her dad's computer. "Danny said we could print as many as we need," she told Cassie.

"Danny!" Cassie exclaimed. "Since when did you start calling your father by his first name?"

"Natalie always calls her mother Lara," Michelle explained. "Don't you think it's . . . sophisticated?"

Cassie shrugged. "I guess . . ."

Michelle clicked "print" on the computer.

"How many invitations should we make?" Cassie asked.

"A zillion!" Michelle said. "I'm inviting *everybody.*"

Invitations began to whoosh out of the printer on thick, gold paper. "Oh, they look great!" Michelle said.

Michelle handed Cassie a pair of scissors. "Now we can start cutting them out. I want them to be in the shape of stars."

"This is going to take forever," Cassie muttered when they were halfway through the star invitations.

"Keep going!" Michelle said. "We need to be done by the time Mandy gets here. She's bringing a bunch of party books so we can decide how to decorate and what kind of food to have."

Michelle had blisters on her fingers when she finished cutting out the last invitation. "Now let's decorate them," she said. "We should use lots of colorful glitter. These have to be the fanciest invitations anybody has ever seen."

"Done!" Cassie announced a half hour later.

"Me too," Michelle said. She gathered up

the sparkly invitations and put them in a shoe box. She couldn't wait to give them out at school the next day.

Michelle heard the doorbell ring. "That must be Mandy!" Michelle said. The girls hurried downstairs.

Michelle placed the invitations on the coffee table, then opened the door. "Did you bring the books?"

Mandy held up her bulging backpack. "My mom had tons of them," she answered.

"Yes! This is going to be the best party ever," Michelle exclaimed. "You have to see the invitations we made."

Michelle led the way into the living room. But the shoe box full of invitations was gone!

"Where are they?" Michelle cried.

"Look under the table," Cassie suggested. "Maybe Comet knocked them on the floor or something."

Michelle got down on her knees and looked. "They aren't here!" she groaned.

Joey came through the front door with two bags of groceries. "What's up?" he asked.

"We made these incredible party invitations—and now we can't find them!" Michelle wailed.

"Look in unusual places," Joey suggested. "I always start with the refrigerator." He headed into the kitchen with the groceries. "Not in here!" he called out a couple minutes later.

Danny came downstairs with a basket of laundry.

"Danny!" Michelle exclaimed. "Have you seen a shoe box full of invitations?"

"I know Natalie calls her parents by their first names. But I *like* to be called Dad," her father said.

"Dad, have you seen my invitations? I left them right here on the coffee table."

Joey wandered back into the living room with a thick sandwich in his hand. "Can't you print out some more?" he asked.

"That will take too long," Michelle cried. "It took hours for us to make them. If we start over we won't be done in time to give them out in school tomorrow. And kids will start making other plans—"

"Okay, okay," Danny said. "Everybody spread out. We don't stop until we find those invitations."

Joey grabbed Danny's arm. "We'll start in the basement and work up."

"I'll start at the top and work down," Michelle said.

"Mandy and I will search the middle," Cassie said.

Michelle dashed to the stairs. Halfway up she noticed something sparkling on the carpet. Glitter.

She followed the trail of glitter to the hall and up the stairs to the twins' room.

Michelle pounded on the door. "Alex! Nicky! Are you in there?"

The door swung open. Alex poked his

head out. His chicken pox spots were fading. But his nose was covered with glitter.

Michelle stuck her fists on her hips. "Have you guys by any chance seen a shoe box full of invitations?"

Nicky peeked out from behind his brother. "What do they look like?"

Michelle brushed the glitter out of his shaggy blond hair. "Paper stars with glitter all over them."

"You mean these?" Nicky asked.

Michelle followed them into their room. And gasped!

Her beautiful invitations were dumped in a pile on the boys' floor. Michelle gathered them up. They still had their glitter. Only a few of the star tips were bent.

That was a close one. Michelle let out a sigh of relief. She stared at her invitations. They were so pretty. This is going to be a really great party, Michelle thought. Natalie and the kids at school are going to love it.

Chapter 7

♡ "Put goat cheese on the list," Michelle said.

"Yuck!" Cassie exclaimed. But she wrote it down.

"I think that's everything we'll need to make the party food," Mandy said.

"Give me the list. Aunt Becky promised to take me grocery shopping tonight," Michelle told them.

Michelle, Mandy, and Cassie sat around the Tanners' kitchen table the next day after school. All the party books were spread out in front of them, along with pieces of silver ribbon, toothpicks, and scissors.

"The next thing we need to do is make the table decoration." Michelle checked the kitchen clock. "The fruit should be dry by now. Our party preparations are right on schedule!"

"I'll go get it," Cassie volunteered. She headed out to the garage where the girls had spray painted a bunch of apples and oranges silver.

"This is how our table decoration should look when it's done." Michelle pointed to a picture of a centerpiece made of a pyramid of silver fruit and ribbon rosebuds.

"Let's start on the rosebuds," Mandy said. She and Michelle picked up pieces of the silver ribbon. They twisted it and folded it, following the directions in the book.

Cassie returned with the silver fruit. She placed it on the table, then she began using the toothpicks to stick the pieces of fruit together.

"This doesn't look much like a rosebud," Mandy said. She held up a mass of tangled silver ribbon.

"Mine either!" Michelle complained.

Thunk! Thunk! Thunk! Cassie's fruit pyramid collapsed. Apples and oranges rolled off the table. "My toothpicks keep breaking!" Cassie moaned.

"Maybe you should use some glue," Michelle suggested. She bent down and helped Cassie collect the fruit. "Oh, no! Some of the paint is coming off."

Orange and red spots were showing through the silver spray paint. "Maybe we can cover up the spots with the ribbon roses," Mandy said. "Or we could stick on some silver glitter."

The phone rang. "Michelle!" Stephanie shouted from upstairs. "It's Lee!"

Michelle dashed over to the kitchen phone. "Hello?"

"Uh, Michelle. It's Lee." He hesitated.

"Um, I called to tell you . . . none of the boys are coming to your party."

"Why not?" Michelle cried.

"Because the invitation says *formal dress!*" Lee exclaimed. "Jeff says his mom says it means we have to wear ties!"

"That's right," Michelle said.

"But how can you have fun all dressed up with a tie and everything?" Lee complained. "You girls don't know what it's like to wear one. It's awful. You can't breathe!"

"But you have to," Michelle told him. "It's important to dress up when you have an important guest like Natalie. Haven't you ever seen Hollywood parties on TV?"

"No way! If we have to wear ties, none of us are coming to your party."

"But, Lee—"

Click!

Michelle stared at the phone. Lee hung up on her!

"Oh, no! My party is ruined!" Michelle wailed.

"Why? What did Lee say?" Cassie demanded.

D.J. rushed into the kitchen. "Michelle! What's wrong? Are you all okay?"

"My party is going to be a disaster!" she cried.

"What do you mean?" D.J. asked. "What happened? Did Natalie have to cancel?"

Michelle flopped back down in her chair. "No. The boys are on strike. They won't come if they have to wear ties. They don't have all-girl parties in Hollywood. Natalie will think we are a bunch of babies."

D.J. sat down next to Michelle. "Don't worry. You've just got to bargain with them."

Michelle sat up. "Like how?"

"Make a trade," D.J. said. "You know, tell them 'If you come to the party, I'll . . .' whatever. Offer them something they really want." D.J. stood up. "Got to go. Good luck!"

"Thanks, D.J." Michelle propped her chin in her hands and looked at her friends. "Any ideas?"

"Hmmm," Mandy said. "What do Lee and his friends like?"

Cassie scrunched up her nose. "Just gross stuff—fake vomit, World Federation Wrestling . . ."

Michelle snapped her fingers. "I just thought of something Lee loves!"

She punched in Lee's number on the phone. "It's Michelle. How about a trade?"

"What do you mean?" He sounded suspicious.

"You do whatever it takes to get the boys to the party, and I'll do something for you," Michelle said.

"Maybe. What?"

Michelle took a deep breath. This was going to hurt. But she *had* to do it. "I'll trade lunches with you for a whole month!"

"All *right!*" Lee shouted. "It's a deal!"

Michelle hung up and made check marks next to all the boys' names on her list.

Phew, she thought. That was another close call. Boy, having a fancy party sure wasn't as easy as she thought. Not easy at all.

Chapter 8

♥ After supper that night Aunt Becky took Michelle to the grocery store. Michelle wasn't used to shopping for fancy food. Some of the stuff was hard to find.

But she finally spotted what she was looking for. Caviar! That's what rich people on TV ate.

The jars were so tiny. Even smaller than baby food jars. "I'd better get a whole bunch of them," Michelle told Aunt Becky. She started to toss some in her cart.

"Hold on, Michelle!" Aunt Becky took a jar from Michelle's hand and held it up. "Do you have any idea what this stuff is?"

"Not really," Michelle admitted.

Aunt Becky pointed at the label. "Look!"

Michelle squinted at the tiny type. "Fish eggs? Ewwww!" She quickly put the jars back on the shelf.

"Don't you think your friends would rather have franks and fries?" Aunt Becky asked. "And brownies."

Michelle loved Aunt Becky's brownies. But they weren't fancy enough. "I don't think they serve brownies at Hollywood parties," Michelle said.

Michelle wheeled the cart down the aisle. She passed bags of cheese popcorn and her favorite taco chips. They weren't special enough for Natalie.

She pointed to the next item on her list. "Do you know where this is? I don't know how to say it. P-A-T-E."

"That's French. You pronounce it pah-TAY. I bet you don't know what it is either," Aunt Becky teased.

"Um, no, I don't," Michelle admitted.

"Goose liver spread."

"Ewwww! That sounds gross!" Michelle said. "I bet Natalie likes it though. I'll just get a little package."

At last Michelle had everything on her list. She pushed the cart up to the checkout line.

"Are you sure you have enough money?" Aunt Becky asked.

"Of course!" Michelle replied. "Dad gave me some, and Mandy and Cassie both loaned me some of their allowance. I told them I'd pay them back when I got mine."

The cashier totaled her purchases and told Michelle the price. Michelle blushed. "Um, Aunt Becky . . ." Michelle said.

"Don't worry, kiddo," her aunt said and then grinned. "I've got some money."

Whew! I almost had another disaster, Michelle thought.

Friday afternoon Michelle, Mandy, Cassie, and Lee gathered in the Tanner kitchen. They tied on big white aprons. Michelle lined up all the groceries she had bought on the counter.

"So, you guys know what you're doing?" Jesse asked Michelle and her friends.

"Sure!" Michelle said. "I help Danny—I mean Dad—in the kitchen all the time."

"And my mom's teaching me to cook too," Cassie added.

"Da-a-a-d!" Alex shouted from upstairs. "Help! Can you come fix this?"

Jesse dashed to the door, then turned to Michelle. "I'll be right back. Don't use the oven or anything. Call me if you need help."

"Go! We'll be fine," Michelle assured him.

Jesse left, and Michelle propped up one of the fancy party books. "I'm going to try to make this three-layer cake that's on the cover," Michelle said. "Isn't it cool how each layer is a different flavor?"

"I would like it better if it were all chocolate," Lee said. "Who wants all those weird flavors?"

Michelle ignored him. "Mandy is making the dip. Cassie is doing the banana pudding. And Lee—"

"I'm the official taste tester," Lee interrupted.

"Uh-uh!" Cassie said. "You can help me mush the bananas."

Michelle and her friends went to work. Soon eggshells, chocolate spills, and banana peels covered Danny Tanner's spotless kitchen counters. And there was flour everywhere.

Michelle whipped up the cake batter and poured it into pans. Then she turned around and checked on her friends.

Mandy held up a bowl full of mushrooms. "Are you sure you want mushrooms in this dip?" she asked. "I don't know many kids who like mushrooms."

"If it's in the book, put them in," Michelle answered.

Mandy stirred in the mushrooms. Then spooned a glob of gray dip onto a cracker.

Lee popped the cracker in his mouth and chewed. "Tastes . . ." His face turned red. He ran and spit into the sink. "Awful!"

"It's okay," Michelle told Mandy. "Lee doesn't know what this food is supposed to taste like."

Michelle picked up another party book. "I'm going to try making these cheese thingies next."

Cassie turned on the blender. Yellow goo gushed everywhere. It splattered on the party books. It splashed on the counter, on the floor, and on the walls.

"You forgot to put the top on!" Michelle yelled.

"Hi, everybody. I'm home!" Danny poked his head into the kitchen.

Splat! A big glob of yellow goo hit Danny in the face.

Cassie winced. She turned off the blender.

Danny wiped his face with a dish towel. He looked as if he were going to faint. "My . . . my beautiful kitchen! Where's Jesse?"

Jesse poked his head in the door. "Hi, Danny. What's up?" Then his eyes popped when he saw the kitchen. "Uh-oh . . ."

"Jesse, you were supposed to watch them!"

"Dad, can I put my cake in the oven?" Michelle asked.

"Go ahead," he said.

"Well, uh, I was," Jesse stuttered. "Sort of."

Michelle slid the cake pans into the oven. "Turn it up full blast," Lee whispered. "It will cook faster." He twisted the knob up to five hundred degrees.

Michelle glanced over at her father. He stared at the kitchen, horrified.

"Uh, I have to go home now," Lee said.

"Me too." Cassie followed him out the kitchen door.

Mandy helped Michelle pile the dishes in the sink. Then she scooted out the door too.

The twins started shouting again, so Jesse slipped away.

Michelle sat down at the table. Danny wiped off the seat of a chair and sat down next to her.

Michelle gulped. The kitchen did look pretty awful. *Here comes the lecture.*

Danny took a deep breath. He opened his mouth—and then he sniffed. "What smells?"

"Oh, no! My cake!" Michelle rushed over and opened the oven door. Thick black smoke poured out!

Danny grabbed some pot holders and pulled out the cake pans. Michelle turned on the fan over the stove.

"Michelle, what were you thinking? You have the oven set to five hundred degrees!" her father said. He turned off the oven.

Michelle stared at her cake. The layers were lopsided. And burned black! She felt like crying.

Michelle had never had so many things go wrong in such a short time! "Oh, Dad!" she cried. "I'm trying so hard. I wanted everything to be so perfect. But no matter what I do, something goes wrong. First the twins took my invitations. Then the boys said they weren't coming to my party. Our table decoration keeps falling apart. And now all the food is ruined! Natalie is going to wish she had never agreed to come."

"Michelle, calm down," Danny said. "Natalie isn't coming over for a fancy party. She's coming over because you two are friends and she thinks it will be fun to see you. Just the way Cassie or Mandy would. Stop trying so hard."

"But I have to have some kind of food at the party." Michelle stared around the kitchen. "We didn't make one thing anyone could eat."

"Don't worry," Danny said. "Super Dad is here." He rolled up his sleeves and slipped on an apron.

"I'll get Uncle Jesse to take everybody out for pizza for supper," Danny said. "Then we'll get to work."

"Can we make the special cake?" Michelle asked. "And the—"

"Yes. But remember what I said. Having fun is the important thing about a party."

Michelle smiled. Her dad was great! But she wasn't sure even *he* could fix this mess!

Chapter 9

 Michelle woke up.

It was Saturday the tenth! The big day!

Her forehead wrinkled with worry. There was still so much to do.

She ran downstairs and vacuumed the living room. Then she raced around putting up all the decorations: the sparkly silver table decoration—it was a little lopsided, but Michelle thought it looked pretty good. A bunch of helium balloons. And a huge glittery banner Michelle and her friends had made that said WELCOME NATALIE!

"Michelle!" her dad said. "Slow down a little. And smile! A party is supposed to be fun!"

"I can't help it," Michelle replied as she zipped past him into the kitchen. "I'm nervous!"

At last it was time to change her clothes. Michelle slipped on her cool new dress. It was all pink and lacy.

Stephanie loaned Michelle some black shoes with high heels. She had to stuff the toes with tissue paper to make them fit.

D.J. put hot curlers in Michelle's hair. Then she tied the curls up on top of her head with a silky pink ribbon.

Now all Michelle had to do was put the food out. She rushed downstairs to the kitchen. She grabbed a pitcher of punch from the fridge and carried it into the living room.

"You look great!" Aunt Becky exclaimed.

"Uh, honey, can I help you with that?" Danny asked.

Michelle shook her head. "I've got it!"

"Ruff! Ruff!" Nicky let Comet out of the

basement! He bounded into the living room—straight for his favorite person.

Michelle!

"Come-e-e-e-t!"

Michelle teetered on her high heels. She dropped the punch—

Splash!

All over her brand new dress!

All over the living room carpet!

"Oh, no!" Michelle wailed at the latest disaster.

Aunt Becky grabbed her key chain. It had a silver whistle on it. *Fweet!* "Red alert! All hands on deck!"

Michelle's family came to the rescue.

Jesse and Joey ran in. They moved the snack table over the spill. The long white tablecloth covered the spot.

Danny tossed Aunt Becky a bottle of club soda. Then he threw one to Joey. "This will take the stain out!" he called.

Aunt Becky and D.J. hustled Michelle to

the laundry room. They yanked off the dress and rinsed it with club soda.

"Is the punch stain coming out?" Michelle asked. "I don't have anything else to wear. None of my other clothes are fancy enough!"

"It's out!" D.J. answered. She popped the dress into the dryer.

The doorbell rang just as Michelle pulled the dress back over her head. She dashed to the front door.

It was Cassie and Mandy.

"Oh, Michelle!" Cassie gasped.

"Everything looks awesome!" Mandy said.

Michelle caught her breath and looked around. Her friends were right. The food, the decorations—everything looked perfect! She could hardly believe it!

Soon the other guests began to arrive. Michelle had never seen her friends so dressed up. Lee had come through. The boys were there—and they were wearing ties!

"So where is she?" Lee asked.

Michelle laughed. "Lee! It's a surprise party, silly. I asked everybody to be here a half hour early. Natalie will be here at one o'clock. Go have some food." She pointed to the snack table.

"Okay," Lee said. He wandered away.

Michelle put on some cool music. Her guests seemed excited. Michelle could tell the party was going to be great!

"I've never met anyone famous before! Do you think she'll bring Brad Pitt with her?" Ann Greene squealed.

"I brought my autograph book!" Cassie said.

Jeff Farrington held up a camera. "Do you think she will let me have my picture taken with her?"

Michelle peeked out through the curtains of the front window. Natalie would be here any minute. She couldn't wait!

"Do you think she could get us free tickets to her movie?" Jeff asked.

"Does she look just like her pictures?" Lucy Tibbons asked.

Michelle peeked out the window again. No sign of Natalie. She was late.

"So where is this Natalie?" a fifth-grade boy asked.

"Maybe she's not really coming," another boy cracked. "Maybe Michelle is trying to fake us out."

"I'm sure she'll be here any minute." Michelle forced a smile. But she was worried.

Michelle checked the clock. Almost one-twenty.

Natalie was twenty minutes late. Had something happened? What if Natalie forgot?

What if Natalie wasn't coming at all?

Ten minutes later, the phone rang. Danny answered it. Then he came into the living room. "Could somebody turn down the music, please? I have some bad news."

Oh, no! Michelle thought. I never should

have had this party. *Everything* has gone wrong.

"Natalie's plane was delayed. It just arrived at the airport. But she *is* coming. She should be here soon."

The kids cheered. So did Michelle.

About half an hour later Mandy grabbed Michelle's arm. She had to shout over the music and laughter to be heard. "Michelle! Wasn't that the doorbell?"

"The doorbell!" Michelle cried. "It must be Natalie! Quick! Turn off the music! Quiet, everybody! She's here!"

"Hide!" somebody squealed excitedly.

Kids ducked behind chairs and curtains. Lee squeezed under the coffee table. Three girls jammed into the hall closet.

Michelle ran to the front door just as Danny came out of the kitchen. "Okay, everybody! Shhh!" Michelle ordered. She opened the door.

Natalie and her mother stood on the front steps. "Hi, Michelle!" Natalie said. She was wearing jeans and a sweatshirt. And she had a couple of beat-up duffel bags with her.

Michelle giggled in nervous excitement. "Hi, Natalie!"

Danny came up beside Michelle and reached to shake Lara's hand. "Nice to see you again, Lara. Do you want to come in and have some coffee?"

"I'd love to," Lara said. "But I'm late." She handed Danny a slip of lavender note-paper. "Here's the number of the hotel where we'll be staying. We're having our meeting there. Sorry I have to run!"

"No problem," Danny said.

Lara gave Natalie a quick hug. "Have a good time, honey. Be good!" With that she flew down the steps to her taxi.

Danny grabbed Natalie's bags and took them upstairs.

"Come on!" Michelle said. She dragged her friend into the middle of the living room. Natalie stared at the decorations and food. "Is somebody having a party?"

"Yes!" Michelle exclaimed.

"SURPRISE!!!" everyone shouted.

Natalie jumped a foot in the air.

"It's a surprise party—for you!" Michelle grinned. Then she turned to her friends. "Allow me to introduce Hollywood's newest, biggest star. Please welcome the fabulous Natalie Campbell!"

Michelle began to applaud. Her friends clapped and cheered.

At first Natalie was speechless. Then she smiled and answered everyone's questions. She signed autographs. She posed with kids for photographs.

Natalie must be having a great time! Everyone wants to talk to her. All my hard work paid off, Michelle thought.

"Oh, Michelle!" Cassie exclaimed. "This is so cool!"

Michelle beamed. They're right, she thought. My party's a total success! Too bad *People* magazine can't be here!

Finally Natalie signed the last autograph.

She posed for the last picture. Jeff Farrington started telling her about a great idea he had for a movie. Now I can have a chance to talk to Natalie myself, Michelle thought. She squeezed between Jeff and her friend. "Are you hungry?" she asked Natalie. "We have pâté—"

"Michelle," Natalie interrupted. "I don't want pâté—whatever that is. I want to go home!"

Chapter 10

♡ Michelle was stunned. She pulled Natalie into the kitchen—away from Michelle's friends. "Why do you want to go home? Do you feel sick? I could get you an aspirin—"

"I'm not sick," Natalie interrupted.

"Then what's wrong?" Michelle asked. She stared at Natalie. Natalie's face was flushed. Her eyes looked wet and she kept blinking. Was she about to cry? "What's *wrong?*" Michelle repeated.

"You should have told me about the party. I thought you liked me for *me!*" Natalie said.

Michelle was so confused. "What are you

talking about? Of course I like you. Why else would I have invited you here?"

"To show off! To prove to your friends that you know someone famous!" Natalie answered.

Michelle felt her stomach clench. How could Natalie think that? "That's not true. I wanted you to have fun, so I decided to give you a fancy party—like the ones you go to in Hollywood."

"Where's the phone?" Natalie asked. "I want to call my mom so she can pick me up."

"Wait. Just listen to me for a second. That day on the beach, we had fun, right? Remember how we—"

"Michelle, bring Natalie back!" someone yelled from the living room.

"She'll be there in one minute!" Michelle answered.

Natalie shook her head. "At the beach you didn't know I was in the movies. Now you do—and that's all you care about!"

Danny rushed into the kitchen with an empty pitcher. "Well, Natalie, having a good . . ." His voice trailed off and his smile disappeared when he saw Natalie's face.

"Mr. Tanner," Natalie said quietly. "Would you call my mom, please? I want to go home!"

"Natalie," Michelle said. "Wait, listen—"

"Please, Mr. Tanner?"

"What's wrong, honey?" Danny asked. "Is there something I can do—"

"No, thank you, Mr. Tanner." She tried to smile. "I'm—I'm just not feeling well. Would you call her? Please?"

Danny's gaze moved back and forth between the two girls. "Well, okay. If you're sure."

"I'm sure." Natalie sniffed. "I think I'll go get my bags now." She ran to the stairs.

"Natalie!" Michelle started to follow her.

But Danny caught her arm and pulled her to a stop. "Want to tell me what's going on?" he asked gently.

Michelle plopped down in one of the kitchen chairs. "She thinks I just threw this party to impress my friends. To show off that I knew a movie star. But it's not true," Michelle wailed.

"Really?" Danny asked. "Not even a little?"

Michelle thought about it. She remembered how excited she felt when she came up with a way to *prove* she knew Natalie. "Well . . . okay. I was mad at some of the kids when they didn't believe I knew her," Michelle admitted. "It felt good to show them that I did. But, honest, Dad, mostly I just wanted to impress *her!* I wanted her to have a good time."

"Next time stop and really think about the other person," Danny said. "Then decide if you're trying to do something for them—or yourself. Natalie goes to fancy parties all the time. She was probably looking forward to something more casual, with no autographs to sign or questions to answer."

He patted Michelle's back. "I guess I better go call Natalie's parents."

I really blew it! Michelle thought. How could I have made such a mess of everything?

"Hey! Michelle!" Mandy stuck her head in the kitchen. "Everybody wants to know where Natalie is."

Michelle hurried into the living room. She felt awful inside. But she pasted a big fat smile on her face. Now, that's acting! she thought.

Michelle grabbed a plate of snacks from the table. "Care for a cheese thingie?" she asked Arlene.

Arlene and a boy named George stared at the plate. George wrinkled his nose. "Got anything *good* to eat? All this stuff is gross."

"Uh—I'll check." Michelle rushed around the room stuffing snacks into friends' hands. If I keep their mouths full, maybe they won't ask about Natalie, she thought.

"Hey," Lee called out. "Where did Natalie go?"

Everybody stared at Michelle. "She's . . . upstairs," Michelle said. "She, uh, had to call her agent."

"There she is!" Jeff called.

Michelle whirled around. Had Natalie changed her mind? Was she coming back to the party?

No. She headed for the front door. Danny followed with her duffel bags.

"Natalie!" Michelle shouted. She pushed through the crowd. But Natalie didn't look back as she hurried out the door.

"What did you do, Michelle?" Arlene sneered. "Insult her or something?"

"Of course she didn't," Mandy cried.

"The food probably made her sick," José called out.

"I-I think she has to run off to an audition or something," Michelle fibbed. "She'll be back later."

Michelle felt sick. She wished the party

was over. She wished it was time for her guests to go home.

Michelle knew she made a fool of herself in front of Natalie and everyone from school.

But worst of all, she made Natalie feel bad. Would Natalie ever forgive her?

Chapter 11

When the last guest finally went home, Michelle flopped down on the couch. "What am I going to do? Natalie hates me!" She buried her face in a throw pillow. "Aaaaggghh!"

Stephanie sat down beside her. "I guess you went a little overboard with the party, huh?"

Michelle nodded. "But I thought that's what she was used to. I thought it would impress her. And . . ."

"And what?" Stephanie asked gently.

"I guess I felt like I wasn't good enough to be friends with somebody special like her."

"Oh, Michelle!" Stephanie said. "You know that's not true. Think about when you met Natalie at the beach. She didn't act all snobby and snooty then, did she?"

"No," Michelle admitted.

"She had a great time hanging out with you—spitting watermelon seeds and playing in the ocean."

"Yeah . . . I guess," Michelle said.

"So why don't you just call her and tell her you're sorry. That's what you would do with Cassie or Mandy." She yanked playfully on the ribbon in Michelle's curly hairdo.

"You just gave me a great idea!" Michelle raced to the phone to call Natalie and ask her to come back over.

"I'm sorry, Michelle," Lara said. "Natalie can't come to the phone right now." Michelle could tell by the way Lara said it that Natalie just didn't want to talk to her.

But Michelle wouldn't give up. "Please, Lara! It's really important. I—I want to apologize to her."

Lara hesitated. "Okay. Hold on a minute."

A few minutes later Natalie came to the phone. "Hello?" Her voice sounded unfriendly.

"Natalie, I'm really sorry," Michelle said. "You were right. I was trying to impress my friends by proving I knew you. But I really thought you would like a big Hollywood-style party. Now I know I made a big mistake."

Natalie didn't say anything.

"I really want to make it up to you," Michelle went on. "Can you please come over and spend the night?"

"No, thanks."

"Puh-lease?" Michelle begged. "It has to be better than sitting around the hotel with your parents, right?"

That made Natalie laugh. "Okay," she agreed finally. "Let me ask Lara." A minute later she said, "I can come. They can bring me over around seven o'clock."

"Great! See you then!" Michelle hung up. *Yes!*

But now she had a lot to do to get ready. She had people to call. Everything was going to be just perfect!

Natalie was really going to be surprised this time. This was a party she would *never* forget!

At seven o'clock a taxi pulled up at the curb. Michelle ran out to the car. Danny invited Lara and Roger into the kitchen for coffee. Laughing and talking, the grown-ups went inside.

Natalie scuffed the toe of her sneaker on the sidewalk.

Michelle held her breath. She hoped this was going to work! Shyly she picked up Natalie's bag and led the way inside. "Come on! I've got a surprise for you."

"Oh, no!" Natalie started to back out the door.

Michelle grinned. She grabbed Natalie's arm and pulled her into the living room.

No one was there.

Natalie laughed. "I thought it was another party for a minute!"

"It is!" Michelle said. "Come on. It's upstairs."

Natalie frowned as Michelle dragged her up the stairs. She shoved open the door to her room. "Surprise!"

Natalie dropped her bag. Michelle could tell she was *really* surprised this time.

The only other "guests" were two very special people—Cassie and Mandy. They both had on shorts and T-shirts. Big beach towels were spread on the floor and both beds. Plates of snacks were set out on the dresser. The shells Michelle collected at the beach were scattered everywhere.

"It's a beach party! An all-night beach party!" Michelle told her. She punched on her cassette player and an old Beach Boys song filled the room. Jesse found the tape for her.

"You remember Cassie and Mandy, right?" Michelle continued, talking as fast as she could. "They are my best friends. You'll like them. They won't ask for your autograph or anything, I promise. We're going to make friendship bracelets later. And teach you our secret code. We can use it in our letters to each other. Do you want a piece of watermelon—or a peanut butter roll-up? They taste almost like peanut butter sandwiches."

Michelle stopped talking. She looked at Natalie and held her breath. What would she say? Would she be mad?

Natalie dropped her bags. "All right!" she cried. She grabbed a peanut butter roll-up and took a big bite. "Delicious," she mumbled.

Michelle let her breath out in a *whoosh!* She smiled at Natalie.

"We forgot to bring the soda upstairs," Cassie said.

"We'll be right back," Mandy told Natalie.

Before Michelle had time to say another word, the twins came barreling in. "Look, Nicky. There's that girl!"

Alex and Nicky stared at Natalie. "We know you," Alex said. Nicky nodded hard.

Oh, no! Michelle thought. It's happening again! Natalie doesn't want people staring at her.

Natalie grinned. "Did you see me on TV?" she asked the boys.

Alex shook his head. "Nope. In our mermaid picture." He held up the photo of Natalie and Michelle.

"So that's what happened to my picture!" Michelle said. "You little sneaks!"

"We like it," Alex said. "We put it in our room."

"Okay, guys, bath time!" Uncle Jesse and Aunt Becky came in after the twins.

Aunt Becky handed Michelle a pan wrapped in foil. "I made you guys a special snack," she said. "Good night."

Michelle peeled back the foil.

Natalie peered over her shoulder. "Brownies!" Natalie cheered. "My favorite!"

"Mine too!" Michelle set the pan on her dresser. "Umm, this is for you." She picked up a juice jar with a piece of paper in it and handed it to Natalie.

Natalie unscrewed the top and pulled out the note. " 'Dear Anyone!' " she read. " 'HELP! I lost my friend Natalie! Save me!' " Natalie laughed. "I'm here to save you," she told Michelle.

"Yay!" Michelle exclaimed. "But I have to ask you one question first. Just one, okay? Before Cassie and Mandy come back," Michelle said.

"If it's about Brad Pitt . . ." Natalie began.

"It isn't," Michelle promised. "I just wanted to know—are you from Japan?"

Michelle's Friendship Fun Stop!

Having friends makes everything fun. You can play together, make things together, even solve puzzles together. So if you and your best friend are looking for fun things to do you've stopped at the right place! These activity pages are filled with best friend puzzles, games, and crafts. And if your best friend can't come over today, you can have fun doing them by yourself too! You can check your answers to all the puzzles on page 136 of this book.

Friendship Pins

Here are two kinds of pins you can make and share with a friend.

Have-a-Heart Friendship Pins

How do you show a friend you like her? By giving her half of your heart . . . your heart pin, that is! Here's how to make a clay pin at home.

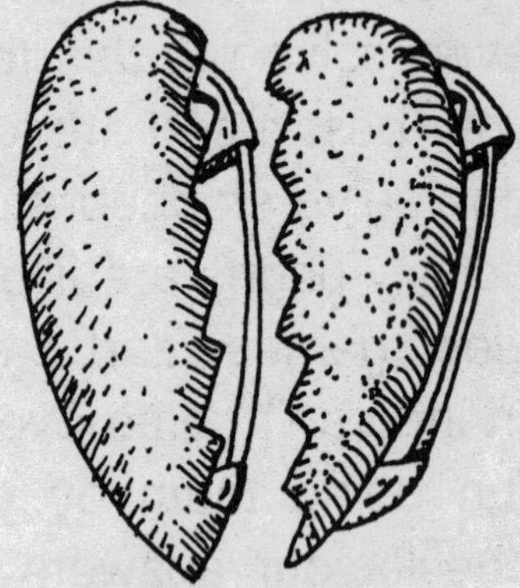

You will need:

2 cups flour
1 cup salt
a mixing bowl
1 cup water
red food coloring
aluminum foil
rolling pin (optional)

butter knife (or heart-shaped cookie cutter)
white glue
2 safety pins
an adult to help

Here's what you do:

1. Mix the flour and salt in the bowl.

2. Slowly add the water.

3. Knead the flour, salt, and water together until they are well mixed.

4. Add a few drops of food coloring and continue to knead the dough.

5. Using your hands or a rolling pin, flatten the dough on a sheet of foil.

6. Ask a grown-up to help you use your butter knife or cookie cutter to cut a heart out of the dough.

7. Ask a grown-up to help you use your butter knife to cut the heart in two with a zigzag line down the middle.

8. Allow the two pieces of the heart to dry completely. Then use a small dab of white glue to attach a safety pin to the back of each half of your heart.

9. Allow the glue to dry before giving your pal her pin.

Now each of you can wear half a heart—and let everyone know you're best buddies!

Sneaker-Pal Friendship Pins

When you and your best friend wear these pins, everyone will get the point—you two stick together!

You will need:

several beads of different colors
2 safety pins (both the same size)

Here's what you do:

Place some beads on the open end of one safety pin, then close the pin. Repeat the same bead pattern on the other pin. Give one friendship pin to a pal and keep the other. Now string one of your shoelaces through the safety pin and wear it on your sneaker.

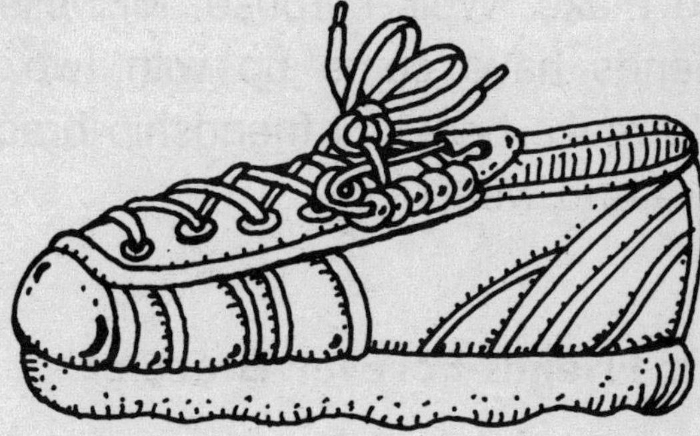

Friendship Bracelets with a Twist!

Have you seen those fun and funky friendship bracelets everyone seems to be wearing these days? We bet you think they are hard to make. Well, surprise! Michelle and her friends have come up with two easy ways to make beautiful friendship bracelets to share and wear!

Friends-Forever Bracelet

You will need:

a ruler
scissors
two 12-inch strings of one color
one 48-inch string of another color
tape

Makes one bracelet.

Here's what you do:

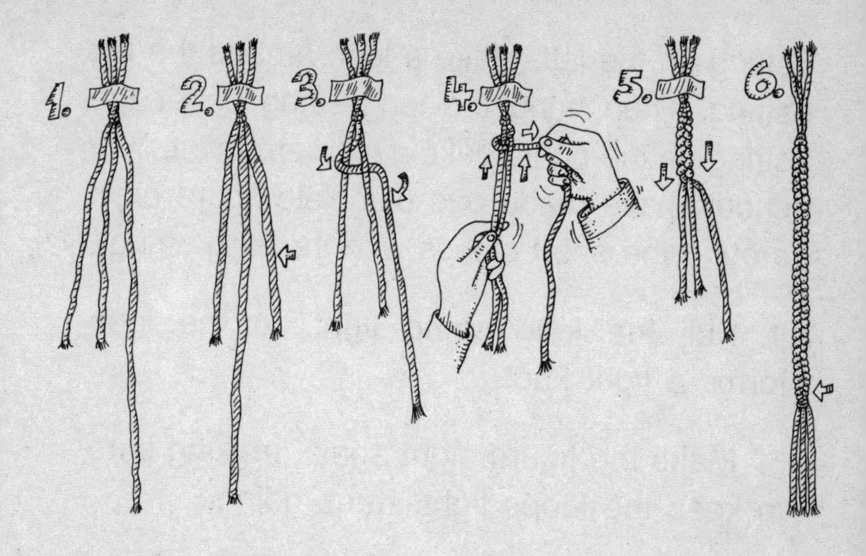

1. Measure and cut two 12-inch strings of the same color, and one 48-inch string of another color. Tie the three strings together at the top with a knot. Then tape the knot to a tabletop or a piece of cardboard (it makes it easier to work with).

2. Separate the strings and arrange them with the shorter strings to the outside.

3. With the long middle string you will make figure eights around the two outside strings. Start by bringing the long string under the

string on the left. Make a loop around the left string. Then bring the long string under the string on the right. Make a loop around it. You should have made one complete figure eight around the short strings with the long string.

4. Pull the long string tight so the loop forms a tight knot.

5. Make the figure eight again, making sure to keep the loops tight. Keep going.

6. When the bracelet is long enough to fit your wrist (remember to leave a little extra room so you can get it on and off), tie it at the end. Wrap the bracelet around your wrist, and tie the two ends together.

Super Best-Friends Bracelet

You will need:

a ruler
scissors

six 30-inch strings, each string of a different color
tape

Makes one bracelet.

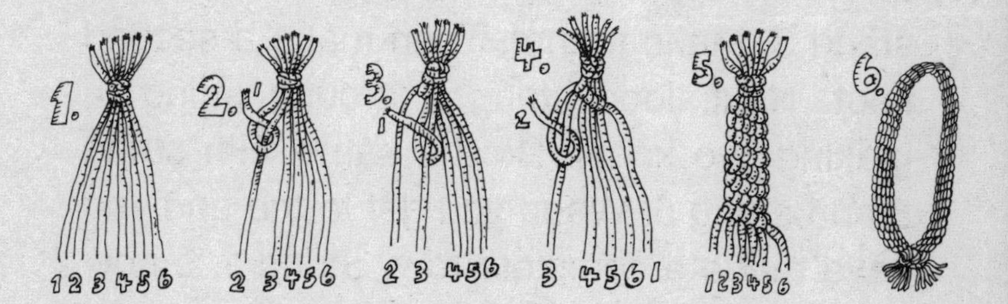

Here's what you do:

1. Measure and cut six 30-inch pieces of string in six different colors. Tie the strings together with a knot about two inches from the top. Then tape the knot to a tabletop or a piece of cardboard (it makes it easier to work with). Separate and straighten the strings.

2. Take string 1 and cross it over then under the string next to it (string 2). You have now made a loop. Tighten the loop into

a knot by holding string 2 and pulling string 1 tight. Make a second knot by looping string 1 over and under string 2 again. Pull string 1 tight.

3. Now loop string 1 over and under string 3. Make a knot. Then make a second knot. Next, loop string 1 around string 4, making two knots. Do the same with string 5 and string 6. When you get to the end you have made a complete row. String 1 is now on the far right.

4. Start again from the left with string 2. Loop string 2 around string 3, making two knots. Continue down the row.

5. Begin the next row using string 3. Keep going, making sure that you always take the strand from the left, and work to the right. And remember to keep your knots tight.

6. When your bracelet is long enough to fit around your wrist (remember to leave a little extra room to slip it on and off), tie a knot at the end. Then tie the two ends together.

Pal Puzzler Surprise!

This jigsaw puzzle will thrill your best friend to pieces! Especially when she puts the pieces together and discovers a picture of the two of you!

You will need:

glue
a photograph of you and your buddy
a sheet of sturdy cardboard
scissors

Here's what you do:

1. Glue your photograph faceup on the cardboard.

2. Use your scissors to trim the cardboard to the exact size of your photograph.

3. Cut the cardboard and photograph into medium-sized jigsaw puzzle pieces.

4. Place all the pieces in a large envelope or small box and give them to your best friend.

*   *   *

A Fun Friendship Book!

You and your best friend are certain to share good memories. But just to make sure you don't forget all the good times you've had together, why not make a friendship book?

You will need:

photos of you and your friend together
lots of little trinkets that remind you of the good times you've had (like ticket stubs from movies you've seen together, maps from amusement parks you've visited, wrapping paper from gifts you've given to one another, or friendship bracelets you've made for each other)
glue stick
construction paper
markers
a hole punch
scissors
yarn

Here's what you do:

1. Spread out all of your photos and trinkets.

2. Choose a photo. See if you can find a few trinkets that remind you of the scene in the picture.

3. Use the glue stick to attach one picture and some trinkets to a piece of construction paper. You might find you have a photo with no trinkets or a trinket with no photo. That's fine! Just paste them on a piece of construction paper and use one of the markers to write about what you and your friend were doing that day.

4. Use your markers to draw pictures or add captions to the page.

5. Repeat steps 2–4 until each picture and trinket is glued to a page.

6. Line all the pages up so they are in an even stack. Use your hole punch to make

three holes on the left side of each sheet of paper.

7. Cut three 6-inch strands of yarn. Feed a strand through each hole, then tie it in a bow.

Now you and your friend can take turns looking through your friendship book and remembering all your special times. And as the good times keep coming, just untie the bows and add more pages.

A Secret Note!

Michelle, Mandy, and Cassie are lucky. They are all in the same class in school. But if your best pal isn't in your school classroom, you might want to leave her a note. The only problem with notes is that other people may find them and read them. But Michelle knows a cool code that's sure to keep your secrets safe.

Use this code box to write your notes:

Rows		Columns 1	2	3	4	5
	1	a	b	c	d	e
	2	f	g	h	i	j
	3	k	l	m	n	o
	4	p	q	r	s	t
	5	u	v	w	x	y/z

To figure out the code, use the row and column numbers to help you find each letter. For example, the letter *o* is in row 3, column 5, so the letter *o* is represented by the number 35. The letter *w* is in row 5, column 3. So the number 53 represents the letter *w*. Since there are only twenty-five boxes, and there are twenty-six letters in the alphabet, the letters *y* and *z* share the number 55, so if you see that number you'll have to guess which of the two letters your friend means to use.

Can you figure out Michelle's message to you?

24 32 24 31 15 12 15 24 34 22
55 35 51 43 41 11 32!

A Letter of Friendship!

What kind of ship never sinks?

Friendship!

How many words can you make from the letters in the word *friendship?* Michelle's given you a few to get you started. Now add your own.

fin

hide

pen

The Best Friends Test!

How well do you know your best friend? How much does she know about you? How about both of you taking this test and finding out?

1. What is your best friend's middle name? ______________________

2. What is your best friend's favorite color? ______________________

3. What is your best friend's favorite TV show? ______________________

4. Who is your best friend's favorite TV star? ______________________

5. What food does your friend like best?

   ____

6. When she grows up, your best friend would like to be a ______________.

7. You and your best friend are going to spend Saturday afternoon together. Which would she want to do most?
   A. Go to the mall and look at the puppies and kittens in the pet shop window
   B. Stay home and watch some scary movies on the VCR
   C. Go for a bike ride and a picnic

8. You and your best friend are going to a party. When you ring her doorbell you discover you are wearing the exact same outfit. What will she do?
   A. Go upstairs and change
   B. Ask you to go home and change
   C. Smile and say she loves it when you dress alike

9. Who is the one person your best friend would like to receive a Valentine from? ______________________

10. When you and your best friend have a fight, which of you is usually the first to say "I'm sorry"? ______________

11. If your best friend could change one thing about herself, what would it be?

____

12. What does your best friend like most about herself?

____

____

13. Is your best friend left-handed or right-handed? ________________

14. You and your best friend are both up for the same role in the school play. Will she:
    A. Decide to try out for a different part
    B. Try out for the same part as you and say "May the best actress win"
    C. Not talk to you until the auditions are over

15. Which of these would gross-out your friend the most?
    A. Kissing the boy who sits closest to her in school

B. Picking up a worm
C. Wearing a frilly lace dress

Now sit down with your friend and check your answers. Give yourself one point for every question you got right.

12–15 points: Wow! You know your best friend like the back of your hand. Maybe even better, since we'll bet you can't remember exactly how many freckles are on the back of your hand!

8–11 points: You and your best friend are closerthanclose! But every now and then she'll say or do something that just might shock you.

3–7 points: You and your best friend are still learning about each other. Maybe this test will help bring you closer.

0–2 points: Are you sure you took this test with your best friend?

My Best Friend's Room Memory Test

How much time do you and your best friend spend in each other's bedrooms? A lot, we'll bet. But how much about your best friend's room do you remember? Take this fun memory quiz and you'll see. When you are through, take a trip to each other's rooms, and check out how you did.

(You and your friend can take this test on the school bus, in the cafeteria, or at the park. In fact, the only place you can't take it is in each other's bedrooms.)

1. How many beds are there in your friend's room? ______________
2. What color is her bedspread? ________
3. How many posters does she have in her room? ______________
4. Does she have any movie star posters? If so, can you name the stars

on the posters? ___________________

____

5. Does she have any animal posters? If so, what animals are on the posters?

____

____

6. Does your friend have any pictures of you in her room? What are the two of you doing in the pictures? __________

7. How many stuffed animals are on your best friend's bed? _________________

8. What color is your best friend's floor?

____

9. What does your best friend keep on her desk? ______________________

10. What color is the chair in your best friend's room? ____________________

11. Are there any signs on your best friend's door? If so, what do they say?

____

____

12. What, besides books, does your best friend keep on her bookshelves?

____

13. What covers the window in your best friend's room?
    A. Blinds
    B. Curtains
    C. A shade

14. How many closets are there in your best friend's room? ______________

15. How many drawers are there in your best friend's dresser? ______________

Telephone Time

Oh, no! It's a rainy day. That means Michelle, Mandy, and Cassie will all have to stay inside. At least they can still talk to one another on the telephone. Can you use your phone to figure out what they are saying?

Look at the numbers below. Then find each number on the telephone. Each number on a telephone has three letters next to it. Try to figure out which letter each number represents. And just to make it a little tougher, each number can stand for a *different* letter each time it appears in the message! (Lucky you! Michelle has helped you out by filling in four letters.)

```
W         b  f                           r
9 3 ' 5 5  2 3  3 7 4 3 6 3 7  3 6 7 3 8 3 7 !
```

* * *

All Booked Up!

What is your best friend's favorite book? Well, you'd better find out, so you can give her this one-of-a-kind bookmark!

You will need:

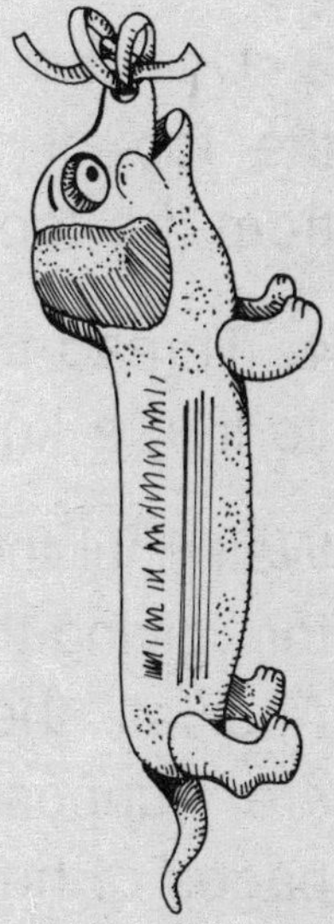

scissors
poster board
a ruler
markers
glitter
glue
a hole punch
ribbon

Here's what you do:

1. Cut out your bookmark from the poster board. A standard bookmark is six inches long, and two inches wide. But you can make your best friend's any size and shape you like. If her favorite book is about a dog,

try a dachshund-shaped bookmark. Be creative!

2. Use your markers to write the title of your best friend's favorite book on the bookmark. Now use the glitter, markers, and glue to decorate the bookmark.

3. Use the hole punch to make a hole at the top of your bookmark, about ½ inch from the top.

4. Thread the ribbon through the hole, and tie it in a knot.

Wait until the glue has dried completely before giving the bookmark to your best friend. After all, the two of you are the ones who are supposed to stick together, not the pages of her book!

Super Snacks!

Are you hungry? Good! Because Michelle and her pals have cooked up a few simple recipes for you to try!

Peanut Butter Roll-Ups

You will need:

a knife
bread
a rolling pin
peanut butter
honey
toothpicks
an adult to help

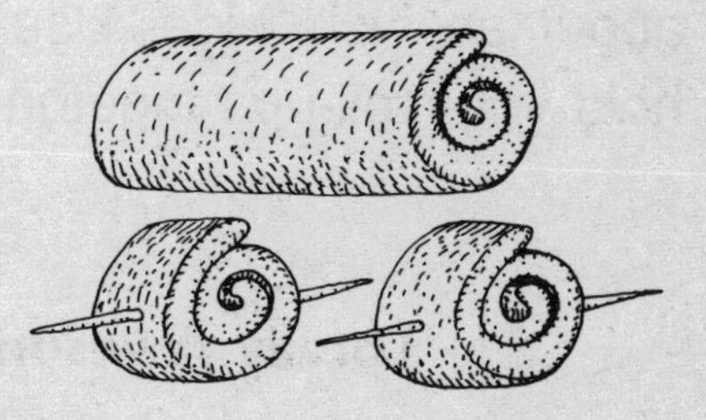

Here's what you do:

1. Cut the crusts off the bread slices with an adult's help. Put each slice of bread on a hard surface.

2. Use the rolling pin to roll the bread out flat.

3. Spread a thin layer of peanut butter on each slice of flattened bread.

4. Spread honey over the peanut butter.

5. Roll each piece of bread from the bottom up so that the peanut butter and honey are on the inside of your roll-up.

6. Ask a grown-up to help you use a butter knife to slice the roll into pieces that are about an inch wide. Use the toothpicks to hold your roll-ups together.

Totally Awesome Fruit

You will need:

chocolate syrup
a bowl
a fork

banana slices
strawberries
apple slices
pear slices
pineapple chunks

Here's what you do:

1. Pour the chocolate syrup into a bowl.

2. Spear a piece of fruit onto a fork.

3. Dip the fruit into the chocolate syrup. Keep dipping and eating until all the fruit is gone.

A Honey of a Treat!

You will need:

1 cup peanut butter
½ cup honey
1 cup raisins
a plastic bowl
1 teaspoon vanilla

1½ cups shredded coconut
wax paper
a tray

Here's what you do:

1. Combine the peanut butter, honey, and raisins in a plastic bowl.

2. Add the vanilla.

3. Mix well.

4. Spread the coconut on the wax paper. Wash your hands. Then pick up a handful of the peanut butter-honey-raisin-vanilla mixture and roll it into a ball. Then roll the ball in the coconut and place it on a tray.

5. Repeat this until all the mixture is gone. Chill the treat for two hours before serving.

Nuttin' Better Drink for Two

You will need:

2 cups milk
4 tablespoons peanut butter

a blender
2 scoops vanilla ice cream

Here's what you do:

1. Pour the milk and the peanut butter into the blender. Blend until mixed well.

2. Add the ice cream, and blend for thirty seconds.

Daring Descriptions!

If I were to describe my friends in a word or two, here's what I'd say:

My friend ______________________________
(name)

is ______________________________

My friend ______________________________
(name)

is ______________________________

My friend ______________________________
(name)

is ______________________________

My friend ______________________________
(name)

is ______________________________

My friend ______________________________
(name)

is ______________________________

My friend ______________________________
(name)

is ______________________________

My friend ______________________________
(name)

is ______________________________

My friend ______________________________
(name)

is ______________________________

My friend ______________________________
(name)

is ______________________________

We Are Alike—
We Are Different!

How alike are you and your best friend? Take this quickie quiz and see how much you have in common!

	Me	My Best Friend
1. Age:	______	______
2. Birthday:	______	______
3. Horoscope sign:	______	______

4. What we look like (circle the correct answer in each row):

	Me	**My Best Friend**
Height	short, tall, medium	short, tall, medium
Eye color	blue, brown, green, hazel, other	blue, brown, green, hazel, other
Hair color	brown, black, red, blond	brown, black, red blond
Hair length	long, short, medium	long, short, medium
Kind of hair	frizzy, curly, straight	frizzy, curly, straight

5. Our personalities (circle the correct answer in each row):

Me	My Best Friend
outgoing/shy	outgoing/shy
funny/serious	funny/serious
messy/neat	messy/neat
cool/nerdy	cool/nerdy

6. Our faves! Fill in the blanks with the things you and your pal like best:

	Me	My Best Friend
color	______________	______________
vegetable	______________	______________
dessert	______________	______________
sport	______________	______________
TV show	______________	______________
actor/ actress	______________	______________
song	______________	______________
singer	______________	______________
book	______________	______________
author	______________	______________
cartoon character	______________	______________

7. These are the school subjects we do well in:

Me

reading
math
science
spelling
geography
computers
art
music
gym

My Best Friend

reading
math
science
spelling
geography
computers
art
music
gym

8. What we want to be when we grow up:

Me

scientist
actress
doctor
nurse
lawyer
police officer
firefighter
dancer
musician
writer
other ____________________

My Best Friend

scientist
actress
doctor
nurse
lawyer
police officer
firefighter
dancer
musician
writer
other ____________________

9. The total:

How many things do you and your best friend have in common? ____________________

Meet My Crowd!

Keep track of your closest buddies. Fill in the blanks.

My best friend is ______________________
My oldest friend is ____________________
My youngest friend is __________________
My newest friend is ____________________
The friend I know the longest is _________
My closest boy friend is ________________
My tallest friend is ____________________
My shortest friend is ___________________
My funniest friend is ___________________
My prettiest friend is __________________
My smartest friend is ___________________
My most talented friend is ______________

Let the Good Times Roll!

Use this page to write about the happiest time you had with your best friend.

Fighting Mad!

Even best pals like Michelle, Mandy, and Cassie have arguments. Use this page to write about an argument you and your best friend have had.

A Trip to the Mall

This is a funny fill-in story. To write this story, gather together a group of friends. Then read them the description beneath the blanks. Write down what they say. Then read the whole story out loud.

Yesterday, Michelle, Mandy, Cassie,

and ______________________ went to the
(name of someone in the room)

mall. It wasn't easy getting there. They

had to ask Michelle's sister D.J. to take

them in her ______________________. At first
(room in your house)

she said, "______________________." But
(a friend's favorite expression)

after Mandy offered to give her

a ______________________, she said "okay."
(a farm animal)

When they got to the mall, Michelle,

Mandy, and Cassie headed straight for

the ________________. They reached out
(name of a thing)

to pet a fuzzy ________________.
(name of a friend's teacher)

"Boo!" Cassie jumped as a

loud ________________ exploded in her
(name of a thing)

ear. It was ________________.
(name of a boy one of your friends likes)

Everyone knew he was the

class ________________.
(the worst thing to be when you grow up)

"You girls should come with me to the

arcade," he said. "We can play a cool

game of ________________.
(name of something that smells bad)

Unless of course you girls

are ________________."
(name of a thing)

That was all Michelle needed to hear. "We're coming," she said. And they all followed him to the arcade.

The inside of the arcade was ______________________ (name of a friend's shampoo). It was hard to see. But Michelle knew just where the game was. She went up to it, put her ______________________ (name of something that tastes bad) in the machine, and the game began.

A crowd of ______________________ (name a type of insect) gathered around. The girls rooted for Michelle, and the boys for ______________________ (the same boy's name you used before).

It was a close game. The score was tied. Michelle used her ____________________ (a friend's favorite thing to wear) to wipe the ____________________ (name of something sticky) from her forehead. Then she pulled back her

____________________ (the part of a friend's body she likes most about herself), aimed, and scored!

Michelle was the winner! She smiled, put out her hand to collect her prize money, and went right to ____________________ (name of a friend's favorite movie), where she bought a brand new ____________________ (name of a thing)!

Answers

A Secret Note!: I like being your pal!

A Letter of Friendship!: Here are some words you can make with the letters in the word *friendship.* How many others did you come up with? Den, dine, dire, dish, end, fend, fried, friend, hind, pie, pin, pride, ship, sip, sire

Telephone Time: We'll be friends forever!